If the Truth Be Known

Greed versus Goodness

A novel

Sara Singleton

ISBN: 978-1-7345197-8-5

Cover design: Marissa Reagan

This book is dedicated with love to my family. To my deceased husband Jack, my daughters Joanne and Suzanne, their husbands Dennis and Brad, and their families. My family is life's greatest blessing, a group that dreams, laughs, plays and loves together.

CHAPTER ONE

She was almost mesmerized by the falling snow as she watched from her bedroom window this early morning in February 2001. Adrianne Paul was recalling a morning like this one many years ago when she was innocent and carefree, playing in the new-fallen snow. What a glorious day that was and curiously remembered so many times in the future. She needed the calming effect of this memory and the falling snow as she awoke this morning in a near panic. So many thoughts had been racing through her head. She was not looking forward to the extremely difficult day ahead. Just another board meeting, she told herself. Go along with their plan. They do not have to know how much you oppose it.

Her husband, Maurice Paul, brought her back to reality as he stirred in his sleep, anticipating their usual wake-up time. The alarm ringing started their morning routine. When Maurice returned from the kitchen with two cups of coffee, he noticed his wife was unusually quiet this morning.

"Good morning, Love. What's bothering you so early this morning?" he asked as he handed Adrianne her coffee.

Adrianne explained that she had not slept well last night.

"I believe that Thomas Gentry, the president of First City Bank, plans a self-coronation ceremony at the board meeting today. He has finally done it. He has confiscated the gem of all banks in the area, got the big prize, the brass ring. In his mind that makes him King of the World. He and his groupies have gone too far. It is unbelievable that these people with so little to offer have so much control! They are all so self-centered and self-serving—their interest is clearly only in themselves, they are about to blow us out of the water."

Adrianne was angry, and her voice showed it as she continued talking. "If this acquisition is approved it will mean an increase in the size of the bank, but these guys have no clue what to do with the bank after the deal is done. This could be my worst nightmare. We do not have the resources to make it work."

Adrianne was also thinking about the major impact on the other bank's employees who would all lose their jobs, and their customers who would also surely be affected.

"Thomas has most of the board members convinced that this is the way to go, that this will certainly increase the value of their stock," she continued. "And for most of them that's what it is all about—more money! What is wrong with all of them? Is everyone crazy or just blinded by greed? We are pilfering a bank and a community. What kind of decision-making is that?" She let out a heavy sigh. "So many mergers these days, it seems we have lost our most endearing values to profit-taking."

"Adrianne, please calm down. You've worked too hard to give up now. Thomas Gentry has built the bank franchise into what it is today. The man has some good points, so give him some credit. Are you sure this won't work? No matter what, you know what the bottom line is here. They cannot do this deal without you. They need you! Just go along with the deal for a while and see how it plays out."

Maurice bent to kiss Adrianne and then held her in a long embrace, as if trying to transfer some of his physical strength to her. The feel of Maurice's body pressed against hers always excited Adrianne but this morning she was disappointed that the desire was quenched by her anxiety.

Maurice quickly dressed for work. His office was only fifteen minutes away in nearby Clarion, but he wanted to get an early start before all the commuters hit the snowy roads. He leaned in for a goodbye kiss. "I'll be in my office all day if you need me."

As she watched her husband pull out of the driveway, Adrianne was much calmer, enjoying the lingering scent of his cologne. She reminded herself how lucky she was to have him as her husband.

It was almost six o'clock when she turned on the TV for the morning news and weather. Even this morning, when she was agitated about the bank, she still wanted to hear what was happening in the world as she started her day. After showering, she took extra time to select her clothes. She always felt more confident when she looked especially good. Looking in the mirror at the finished product, she was pleased with the reflection. Her spectacular shoulder-length red hair complemented her 5-foot-8 slender frame. Her black silk suit by her favorite designer and white silk blouse with a gold necklace completed the look. She wore basic makeup, just enough to accent her fair skin. At 36 years old, she was in the prime of her life. Most people thought she was younger, and all agreed she was quite attractive. Her mother had often told her, "Adrianne, use your looks while you still have them—they are one of your biggest assets."

The clock downstairs chimed seven o'clock as

Adrianne walked into the kitchen for a quick breakfast before collecting all her necessary accessories for work and heading out to brave the wintry morning.

CHAPTER TWO

Adrianne pulled into the First City Bank parking lot a little before eight o'clock and walked in the snow the short distance to the front entrance. The building was quite impressive—twelve stories of gray glass with a small shopping complex on the first floor as well as a First City branch.

"Good morning, Mike. How are you today?" she asked the security guard as she entered the building.

"I am just fine, Adrianne," he replied. "No need to use your security card, you can go right in."

"Thanks. How is your family and your new grandson?"

"The baby is just fine. He looks like his father and the rest of the Eagle men."

"Then I am sure he is a very handsome baby," she said, smiling. "When you get a chance, stop by my office with a picture. I want to see what the newest member of the Eagle family looks like."

Adrianne had a special fondness for Mike as they had both started working at First City on the same day six years ago.

Adrianne walked into the main concourse that housed the largest of the First City branches. She was always delighted to see the branch as she walked past the glass walls that separated it from the rest of the building. This was one of the most elegant and modern branches in the region.

As the retail side of the bank was one of her responsibilities, she had been involved with the planning and development of this branch. She was pleased that it provided technology and customer service far superior to the bank's competitors in the area. As she walked to the elevator, Adrianne greeted several employees and then rode up to her office on the ninth floor. She could see as she walked to the opposite side of the building that some of her staff members were off to an early start.

She stopped outside her office to greet her assistant. "Good morning, Elizabeth. It looks like the weather isn't going to slow down our busy day. Give me five minutes and then we can get started."

Adrianne's office suited her. It was elegantly decorated and comfortable. She deposited her briefcase, coat and handbag in the sitting area and turned to look out the glass wall of her office.

"Elizabeth, look how beautiful the snow is. It's

a winter wonderland. Have you heard a weather report recently?"

"Three to five inches are expected," replied Elizabeth. "Adrianne, if you're ready, I have your board reports for review, some correspondence for your signature and Andrew Morgan wants to see you as soon as you are free. He says it's important."

"I am all yours for fifteen minutes," Adrianne replied.

They had just finished when Andrew opened the door.

"Am I interrupting my two favorite women? Should I come back later?"

"Come in, Andrew. What's this important issue that can't wait?"

Anticipating this was a confidential matter, Elizabeth closed the door as she left.

As operations director, Andrew was responsible for all the support areas as well as technology at First City and was one of Adrianne's most valued and trusted employees. He shared her love for the nuts and bolts of the bank. They spent many long hours together to ensure the bank operations were efficient. Andrew was a good-looking man, over six feet tall with dark brown hair. He walked with a slight limp, which was hardly noticeable. Adrianne often wondered what had caused the limp. The dress code had been changed several years ago to casual, which Andrew reflected with his signature suspenders, white shirt and slacks.

He settled into a chair opposite her. "Adrianne, what I am going to tell you must be kept in strictest confidence. My friend Sam Van Arsdale from Clarion National Bank called me at home last night in a panic. The rumor at their shop is their bank is being sold to us and the announcement will be made today." He paused to let that sink in. "Sam is very concerned about the employees losing their jobs and the fact that this could be a nasty takeover. He knows Thomas Gentry is insensitive and can be extremely ruthless. He also pointed out that most of their employees, as well as the local stockholders, would be vehemently opposed to this acquisition. I told him that I would try to find out what is going on."

"Andrew, you have been through this before with our prior acquisitions. You know that a matter like this is not final until it has both banks' board approval, which is pending stockholders' approval."

Andrew sighed wearily. "I know what you're saying is true, but I am totally frustrated with all these mergers, deals or whatever you want to call them. What is the point to all this madness? Don't get me wrong. It is not about all the extra work we need to do—I don't mind that. What really bothers me is the fact that as we have grown the bank with five acquisitions and more to come, so many people have lost their jobs. Two hundred maybe, with probably three hundred, five hundred or even a thousand more losing their jobs in the future, completely disrupting their lives. And for what? To make a few people wealthy!" He stood up, his anger palpable. "Are these employees the sacrificial lambs to the big corporations? Some of these people have worked a lifetime at their jobs and one day we say 'Okay, your time is up, we don't need or want you anymore. We're sorry but for banks to survive they must be more competitive and that means be big, bigger and biggest.' This is bullshit and you know it!"

Andrew was shouting now and began pacing the floor as he continued his tirade.

"Do you remember Tom Young from Valley Bank? He had worked there twenty-five years when this happened to him. We gave him a nice severance package and said goodbye. He was so devastated that he literally gave up and ultimately lost everything, ending up homeless and living on the streets. Bigger is not better. We are killing the human spirit for the sake of greed! I spent two years in the Army fighting a similar war in another country. I became physically handicapped from that effort—I don't want to become mentally handicapped as well."

"Andrew, please calm down," Adrianne said. "I

had no idea that you felt so strongly about this situation. Personally, I don't like what I am seeing either, but it is our job to support the bank's plans and policies. We try to change what we can and pick our battles wisely." She paused to look at her watch. "Oh, look at the time. Andrew, I need to attend the board meeting in fifteen minutes. Can we continue this discussion later?"

"Sure." He opened the door and paused in the doorway, turning back with a pained expression. "I'm sorry I got a little carried away."

A very concerned Adrianne watched him leave her office. She had never seen him in this state of mind.

CHAPTER THREE

The board meeting was held on the top floor of the bank building. Many of the board members—a mostly male group—had already gathered and were talking in small circles throughout the large board room. As Adrianne walked in, she spotted Bruce Burt, chairman of the board, chatting with a group near the entrance. Bruce was one of her favorite people as well as her mentor. And he's so attractive and distinguished-looking, she thought to herself. Bruce noticed her approaching and extended his hand to welcome her into the conversation.

"Bob, I would like you to meet Adrianne Paul, our executive vice president," Bruce said. "She is responsible for a large portion of the bank, the branches and all our operations. She is not only beautiful but also outstanding in her job."

Adrianne's smile and reverent look at Bruce was her acceptance of the compliment.

"You have quite a following, Adrianne," replied Bob Van Zyl, one of the new board members. "I've heard many good things about you. It's nice to finally meet you."

"Thank you and welcome for the kind words," Adrianne said. "I had heard you were recently appointed to the board. Your expertise as CEO of RV Technology will certainly be an asset to the bank."

Adrianne excused herself and moved across the room, chatting briefly with the other board members including Mark McFall, president of McFall Enterprises, Anthony Rissi, a self-employed architect, Catherine Shearer, marketing director for a local business, and Tim Ward, president of Ward Foundation. She also spotted Larry White, chief financial officer, and Corey Reagan, senior vice president of lending.

In total, there were twelve members of the board including Thomas Gentry and Bruce Bart, and all were involved with the bank in one way or another and with different degrees of intensity. Ever since the laws had changed to make bank directors more liable for losses and infractions of federal regulations, the strength of the board had also improved. Several directors were unwilling to accept the increased responsibility and had chosen to resign. Adrianne thought this had improved the board overall.

The meeting started on time, with Bruce seated at the head of the table and Thomas at the opposite end. Five directors sat on either side of the table, with a row of chairs behind the directors for other non-member attendees. Bruce was an impressive chairman. He knew how to direct a meeting of this significance, maintaining perfect timing in exercising control on all levels to keep the meeting running smoothly and effectively. From Adrianne's vantage point she could see both Thomas and Bruce. What a difference there is between them, she thought.

Bruce was a class act. In his early fifties, he had a striking face with a wonderful smile, almost protruding good character. Bruce was always full of energy and enthusiasm, but what Adrianne admired most was his integrity.

Thomas was quite the opposite—ambitious but ruthless. Younger than Bruce by about 15 years, he was in a great hurry to get to the top. Thomas had poor leadership skills but his biggest asset, or his downfall, was salesmanship. Right or wrong, he could talk most people into doing whatever he wanted. He frightened Adrianne sometimes with the power he seemed to have over people. Thomas was a smooth operator with little virtue.

Adrianne glanced around the room. It was impressive, even compared to other board rooms she'd seen, and she felt this room particularly exemplified corporate America. In the center was an oversized mahogany table that comfortably seated twenty people in overstuffed black leather chairs. The focal point of the room was a beautiful Austrian crystal chandelier that hung directly over the center of the table. Three walls were rich mahogany paneling, and the fourth wall was glass with a wonderful view of the surrounding area. The double doors—the entrance to this sacred corporate room—were also mahogany and as you walked through, a small anteroom greeted you with a grouping of formal furniture resting on a marble floor. Peripheral to all of this was a small kitchen and media area.

Adrianne's attention drifted back to the meeting. Larry White had just finished reading the financial reports and was answering questions. The financial conclusions were that First City Bank was one of the most profitable banks in the East, with excess capital and a balance sheet envied by most of its competitors.

Next up were presentations from Corey Reagan and Adrianne. Directors Jackie McPeak and Sharon Downing were impressed with the glowing reports and led the other board members in appreciative applause.

Thomas Gentry spoke next on the general well-being of the bank and several current special projects. Then he broke the news. "Ladies and gentlemen, I have just finished negotiating an agreement to purchase Clarion National Bank. I believe this is a great opportunity for us. Clarion has 35 branches in the Philadelphia market area and northwest of it. The increase in size will allow First City Bank to be more competitive and profitable with the expansion of our franchise area for lending and retail sales as well as cost savings from consolidation and downsizing."

Thomas continued for another 30 minutes discussing the bank's expected return on the investment and the situation at Clarion National Bank. He said that James Conway, Clarion's president, and his staff had for some time been looking for a suitor to buy the bank. "They all own a considerable amount of stock and stand to become very wealthy with our offering," Thomas said. "Mr. Conway believes he has enough director votes to gain board approval for a merger stockholder vote. Wall Street has told me that if this deal comes to fruition, it will be supported and drive up our stock price."

Thomas then asked for questions or comments from the directors before moving to a vote. Mark McFall was the first to speak up. "This purchase raises the question of shareholder interest versus the rights of employees and customers of Clarion National Bank. Are we jeopardizing the future of the bank for short-term shareholder profit?"

"I'm not aware of any employee or customer rights in this situation," Thomas replied.

The room then erupted into a very heated discussion, which surprised Thomas; he had not counted on opposition from the board. He was relieved when an hour later Bruce asked for a vote.

CHAPTER FOUR

Early every morning, Tom Ryan walked to the end of his driveway to retrieve his local newspaper. Today was no exception, even though the snow from the day before was piled on both sides of the driveway. Tom took his time, negotiating around the ice patches as best he could. On his way back into the house he glanced at the thermometer—18 degrees. "Brr," he said to his dog as they entered the house, "it is cold out there." Tom lived alone; his wife had passed away two years ago.

He was quickly absorbed by the morning news and his first cup of coffee, when he came upon an article about Clarion National Bank. Reading on, it started by stating that Thomas Gentry, President of First City Bank, was pleased to announce that the Board of Directors of the Bank had approved a tentative merger agreement with Clarion National Bank. The article then stated that the acquisition was conditional upon the approval of

Clarion National Bank stockholders and federal bank regulators. Thomas Gentry was quoted as saying that he expected the transaction to take place soon and that he anticipated absolutely no problem with stockholder approval. Tom became more agitated with every word he read.

"Mr. Gentry!" His shout startled awake the dog napping at Tom's feet. "Over my dead body will you culminate this deal. THIS WILL NOT HAPPEN! ENOUGH IS ENOUGH!"

By eight o'clock, Tom had calmed down enough to begin a series of phone calls to organize a meeting of interested parties to stop the takeover of Clarion National Bank.

Early that same morning, Sam Van Arsdale, director of operations at Clarion National Bank, entered his own office. He hadn't slept much and was anxious to start work. He had talked to his friend Andrew Morgan yesterday and confirmed that the rumor circulating around his bank was true. First City Bank did indeed have a tentative agreement to acquire Clarion Bank. Sam felt completely betrayed. How could they sell out like this? So many people had invested so much of their lives in this bank to make it the success it was today. Sam was finally facing the fact that those credentials were not important in today's business environment. Apparently, it was only important to make a few people wealthy and to hell with anyone or anything everything else, especially employees and customers. They had no rights.

What a pathetic state this country is in, Sam thought. The day was starting out to be one of the lowest points in his life.

Shortly after eight o'clock, Sam's thoughts were interrupted by the phone ringing.

"Sam Van Arsdale," he answered.

An extremely agitated voice on the other end of the phone said, "This is Tom Ryan. Have you read the morning newspaper? Of course, you have. I can already tell by the tone of your voice. We are not going to let this happen," Tom said. "We are going to fight back. There is a group of people meeting at the Union Hall tonight at eight to plan a strategy to stop this merger. Can you come?"

"Yes," Sam replied. "I will be there. See you soon."

Sam hung up. His spirits were somewhat lifted. At least someone cares, he thought. Tom was a good friend of his father's; Sam had known Tom since he was a boy. Tom and Sam's father, Art, had worked together for 20 years on the production line at the Corbet Container Corporation where Art was a supervisor. Tom went on to become head of the union. Many of Clarion's residents had owed their livelihood to the company, which employed over 2,000 people until the plant closed five years ago, leaving the town devastated.

Corbet Container had been a local company for 40 years, started by Jason Corbet as a small shop that grew over the years into a national company. Mr. Corbet was greatly respected by his employees and by the community. He had a vision for his company that included valued products, good wages and benefits for employees who shared his vision, worked hard and made a commitment to his customers. He continually sought to improve his manufacturing equipment to make it more productive, safe and cost-effective. He believed that if he could follow this plan his company could generate considerable profit—and it did.

When Mr. Corbet died 12 years ago, his family did not want to run the company, so they sold it to a national conglomerate. This new company wanted more profit. First, they downsized, then they reduced the quality of the products and finally they moved the plant to a location where they could get cheaper labor. The townspeople and the Corbet employees felt betrayed, demoralized and disheartened. They never recovered.

CHAPTER FIVE

Sam was startled when Ashley Kelly abruptly charged into his office. "Oh, Sam, how could they do this?"

Sam sat back a moment and looked at Ashley as if to gather another image of her to store in his memory. Ashley was one of his managers. He had always been enamored with her. Ashley was a beautiful young woman with long red hair and a great figure. She was one of those rare treasures—an unassuming woman who had no idea how she affected men, especially him. Even though she was very intelligent, she was naïve about her looks. Ashley had a wonderful personality, so positive and cheerful, and she found value in everything. If Ashely hadn't already been married, Sam would have liked the chance of dating her.

Right now, Ashley could no longer contain her tears; they were like waterfalls. "How could they do this to us?" she sobbed. "They sold us out and now we have nothing."

Sam came out from behind his desk and took Ashley in his arms to comfort her. His emotions for her were stronger than his feelings for the situation, and he could hardly contain himself being so close to her.

Ashley's sobs had been overheard by some of Sam's staff and soon several people had gathered at his office door to see what was happening. Ashley quickly broke away from Sam's embrace, somewhat embarrassed.

Sam's assistant came to the rescue and announced that Mr. Conway, the bank president, had emailed all employees a schedule of meetings to be held today to discuss an important issue. With the active grapevine at the bank, most of the employees already knew what the important issue was, but they were still anxious to hear what the president had to say.

At ten o'clock, about 40 people gathered for the first meeting. Flanked by two of his executive officers, Mr. Conway confirmed there was indeed a merger agreement pending with First City Bank and Clarion National Bank, with First City being the survivor. The Clarion Board of Directors had given their vote of approval late the night before, and stockholder and regulatory approval were expected within sixty days. He explained hat the board felt it was in the best interest of the bank and the community to combine resources with First City through this merger to stay competitive in the marketplace and defer the increasing cost of technology.

"Stop insulting our intelligence with this garbage!" Gerald Detrick, a long-time employee, shouted angrily. "What you've done is tantamount to signing a death warrant on this bank. You were never interested in this town or these people. Your only interest since you came here has been to sell this bank and make a nice profit for yourself and your cronies. How can you stand up there in front of all of us and say this is in the best interest of our community, when most of us will lose our jobs and the town will lose its bank? Mr. Conway, I know one thing that I can do as a shareholder. I will vote 'no' for this merger, and I will actively seek out other stockholders to do the same."

The audience broke out in applause.

"One more thing, Mr. President," Gerald continued. "Don't even think about terminating me. We both know that everything I have said here is true and if I am fired you will have a major lawsuit on your hands. I intend to remain here if only to remind you of what you have done."

James Conway was seething under his calm façade and motioned to the security officer to remove Gerald Detrick from the room. The security officer turned his head at the same time

Conway looked his way and did not acknowledge his request.

Conway had anticipated some problems but not to this extent. This was his deal—he had carefully solicited, managed and nurtured this sale. He was not about to lose it over these people. He wanted acceptance at these meetings. He felt he could accomplish that at least with most employees. He knew that he needed some of these people to ensure a smooth transition.

Conway believed he was far superior to his employees and, so far, it had been relatively easy to convince them to do whatever he wanted. At this point, he did not care what they thought. In his mind, they were just pawns, and nothing could stop the deal now.

Knowing he could do nothing more with this audience, he charmingly feigned another urgent matter and turned the meeting over to one of his executives.

CHAPTER SIX

Sam Van Arsdale had enough for one day, maybe enough for a lifetime. At four o'clock he left the bank and headed home. On a day like today he wished he had a wife to go home to; he desperately needed to talk with someone. He frequently stopped to visit with his parents on his way home and today seemed a perfect opportunity to do just that.

Sam was an average-looking guy, in his mid-thirties, almost six feet tall with brown hair and hazel eyes. To his credit, he was meticulous about his appearance and clothing. Along with being a perfectionist, he was also very intelligent and intuitive, and everyone who knew Sam said his personality was one of his biggest assets. He was an outgoing person with a great sense of humor who was also very caring.

Sam always felt reminiscent as he pulled into the driveway of the home in which he had grown up. He walked into the kitchen through the back door and greeted his mother. She was preparing dinner as she had so many times when he lived there.

"Sam," Carolyn said as she greeted her son, "will you stay for dinner?"

She could immediately sense that something was wrong. At that moment Sam's father, Art, entered the kitchen.

"I thought I heard your voice, son. How are you?"

Over dinner, Sam shared the events of the last few days, telling his parents he had no idea that he could feel so completely betrayed and depressed and that he had deep concerns for all the other bank employees who were feeling these same emotions. It was a relief to unload his anger and disappointment.

"How do I cope with this?" he asked.

Art told him that he understood exactly how he was feeling. He experienced the same emotions years ago when the Corbet Container Corporation was sold.

"One day everything is fine and then the next your life unexpectedly explodes and you hit rock bottom," Art said. "You are now looking for the pieces to put your life back together again. But you're young and strong, son. Even though your life is about to change drastically, you will find the strength to get through. I know one thing. You must take this experience and learn from it, grow with it. You must move forward. Don't become bitter and absorbed in this situation. Maybe now is the time to get more education, try a new field. Whatever you decide, your mother and I are always here for you."

Art patted Sam's shoulder and then continued. "I talked with Tom Ryan today. He filled me in on some of the happenings at your bank. You are right about the executives; they are bastards only looking out for themselves. Tom seems to think there is a good chance to rally the stockholders to vote against the merger. What do you think?"

"It's a long shot, Dad, but worth a try," replied Sam. "What do we have to lose?"

Carolyn noticed that there was a faint sparkle in Art's eyes, something she had not seen for a long time. She remembered how they had all learned first-hand the hard way about companies trading workers' jobs and rights for shareholder gains. When the Corbet Container Corporation closed, the employees' jobs were all gone, and in the end the shareholders didn't fare much better. There was only a small immediate profit after the sale. The outcome of the whole situation was a big loss for all involved. Now they knew better and were ready to fight back. Turning the situation with Clarion National Bank around, Carolyn thought, could return some self-esteem to her husband and some of the townspeople. On the other hand, what would happen if they lost? It was a big risk.

That night, Sam and his father drove together to the town meeting that Tom Ryan had arranged. On the way, Sam asked his father why Tom was so interested in the takeover of Clarion National Bank.

"Tom feels he is partly to blame for what happened to the employees and the town when Corbet Container closed," Art said. "He felt that he should have seen it coming and been prepared to do something to prevent the company from closing.

"Tom and I have been good friends since we went to high school together," Art continued. "I can tell you about some of the events of his life so that you will better understand him. Tom was in his early twenties when his first misfortune happened: the love of his life broke his heart. The young woman he was engaged to was not content to live with him in a small town like Clarion. She tried to get him to move to a metropolitan area, but it was in vain, so one day without warning she left him a 'Dear John' letter and went off to seek a new life for herself. Tom tried for years to find her but finally gave up. Soon after that, Tom became very active in the Corbet Container Corporation Union. He started out as a union steward and worked his way up through the ranks to become its leader. For ten years, his emotional life was transferred to that union. He became a dedicated and dynamic leader, greatly respected by the nearly seventeen hundred members of his union as well as Jason Corbet himself."

Art told Sam that Tom's second misfortune was when Corbet Container Corporation was closed.

"Still, even with all that, Tom did fall in love again in his early forties. He and his wife were happily married for twenty years before she died from cancer and that tragedy was the third misfortune in his life. I believe that in his mind, Tom feels he has lost three of the most important battles of his life and he needs to win this one to redeem himself."

Sam thought about the three misfortunes as they drove to the Union Hall. He hoped he might be able to help Tom feel redeemed about all the bad things that had happened to him.

When Sam and his father arrived at 7:15, a couple dozen people were already there including Tom, who immediately walked toward them. In his early sixties, Tom was an impressive-looking man at over six feet tall with graying red hair.

"Hello, old friends," Tom said as he extended his hand first to Art and then to Sam. "How are you both? Sam, I know you must be feeling low right now. I think we have a fighting chance to turn this thing around. We have some good people coming tonight. Let's see how it goes."

More people were entering the hall and Tom went to greet them.

The meeting started shortly after eight o'clock. Tom was pleased there were about two hundred in attendance; he was good at rallying people to action, a carryover from his union days.

"My friends," Tom began, "thank you all for coming. We are all here to prevent another crime from happening in our community. I am not talking about the usual crimes. I am talking about the theft and extinction of a longtime business establishment in our town. A business that has deep roots in our community, one that was built and flourished using our money. We all invested in Clarion National Bank with our savings and even our children's pennies to make this bank what it is today."

As Tom continued to speak, his tone became more emotional with each sentence.

"It was a good investment because the payback was to the community, to our town and to its people, to grow. Loans from this bank helped our businesses prosper, brought in new business, financed our homes and our cars and helped send our young people to college. To this day, it provides a lifeline to each of us and to our town. I, for one, do not want to see it merged with a bank that cares little for our town and its people and continues the merger process again and again. Ultimately, our bank will become part of a mega bank that places little value on its customers or any communities. We all know what happens with large companies. The demise of Corbet Container Corporation is embedded in all our memories."

Tom paused to collect his thoughts and to ensure he had everyone's attention.

"I have called you here tonight to stop this terrible injustice. It is time for us to act and fight back. Let's show these annihilators that the people have power. We can do anything if we do it together. What do you say, are you with me on this?"

The audience erupted into a standing ovation and shouts of "We're with you, Tom!"

When the room quieted down again after a few minutes, Sam rose and asked Tom how they could stop the acquisition.

"Good question, Sam," Tom replied. "The first action is to contact all Clarion stockholders. Their approval is necessary for this deal to go through. I understand the voting process is being held within two months from the day the offer was received. We must get fifty-one percent of the shareholders to vote no on the bank sale. This will not be easy, but I think it is doable. I suggest that we separate into smaller groups to discuss everyone's ideas and impending contributions to accomplish our goal."

A plan had begun to materialize when the group came back together again an hour later. Sam reported first for his group.

"Our group discussed needing certain critical information to begin this fight, like the date of the stockholder voting meeting and a current listing of Clarion Bank stockholders."

Arnold Baker, Editor in Chief of the Clarion News, spoke for the next contingent.

"I want everyone to know that our newspaper will support this effort and is committed to doing whatever it takes to save our bank. We believe it's necessary to use the power of the press to achieve our goal."

More reports from the small groups followed. Members of the various civic organizations in the area committed to spreading the word through their channels in order to solicit volunteers and cash donations.

Finally, Tom's friends from the locally deposed Corbet Container Corporation Union, represented by Shawn Reagan, reported they still had contacts with the national unions that they could use to focus national attention on the efforts of the community to block the merger. They also discussed doing some detective work on the major players of the deal to gain information helpful to the cause.

These were all important and useful steps, but Tom also knew they would need more than community enthusiasm. They needed a plan.

CHAPTER SEVEN

Tom Ryan rose early the day following the formal announcement of the planned acquisition of Clarion National Bank by First City Bank. This news had prompted him to call a meeting last night at which about 200 Clarion town residents came to discuss community awareness and involvement in stopping the acquisition, and now he was reflecting on how that meeting had gone.

Tom had called the meeting to order and participated as a strong leader explaining the dire situation of Clarion National Bank being sold. He created an electric atmosphere and everyone there became committed to this crusade. He was pleased that the meeting had been a huge success. By the end of the night, all the attendees unanimously agreed that the bank should not be sold, and maybe by working together, they could make a difference and stop this acquisition.

But now Tom thought about the questions he had asked himself as he was falling asleep the night before. How would they stop the acquisition? What was their plan? As part of the acquisition, most of the Clarion National Back branches would remain open, but all operations jobs and management positions would be eliminated. The role of the bank as a corporate leader in the community would also be gone—a huge loss.

As the day progressed, Tom began to formulate a plan. At the meeting, they concluded that the only way to succeed was for fifty-one percent of the Clarion Bank stockholders to vote 'no' on the acquisition. But making this happen was a major project. He could see now that their group needed to organize a steering committee for planning and direction.

He sat down in his lounge chair to contemplate his part in this endeavor. Tom wished that his wife was there to talk with him. She was his love and partner in life for many years; he missed her all the time, especially now. He wondered what she would have said about the situation.

Tom was semi-retired and in his early sixties. He had an active corporate and community life and was well known in the town of Clarion for being a leader and doing the right thing. But this time, Tom wasn't sure if he had the will and energy to help the group achieve their goal. With these thoughts swirling in his mind, he dozed off.

He awoke several hours later and had his answer. He would do whatever was needed to stop the sale of Clarion Bank and the first step was to call his friend Art.

Shortly after dinner the doorbell rang. Tom answered it and found four people there on his porch—the Van Arsdale family (Art, Carolyn and Sam) and Andrew Morgan. Both Sam and Andrew were Directors of Operations for the Clarion and First City banks.

"Welcome all. Come in, come in! How nice to see you. Let's go into my home office, also known as the dining room," Tom said, grinning. "We have lots of room to work at the big table. Please sit down so we can talk. Let's begin by establishing a degree of confidentiality?"

All agreed and Tom continued speaking.

"Andrew, I am surprised to see you as you work for First City. Tell us about your feelings on the bank merger."

Andrew replied that he was totally against it and was volunteering to do what he could to stop it.

"Good," Tom said. "From this point we must be careful to keep our plans undercover, so the wrong people don't find out what we're doing."

After much discussion the group came up with a plan. Establishing a steering committee was the first priority, followed by a meeting with Matthew

Oliver, the chief financial officer at Clarion National Bank, to discuss how best to use the stockholder information. Next was contacting the Editor of the Clarion News to publicize their opposition to the acquisition. The group also agreed there must be an investigation into the president and top management of First City Bank to make sure all their actions were legal.

"And for that," Tom said, "our group needs an attorney."

Sam said he felt this was a good beginning, adding, "Now it's time to go home and we will reconvene tomorrow."

As they gathered their things to leave, Carolyn stayed a little behind and told Tom, "Your wife would be pleased at what you have done."

CHAPTER EIGHT

Matthew Oliver had lived in Clarion all his life and was happily married to Eileen now and raising two children there. As a life-long resident, Matthew was well acquainted with Joseph Clarion, who founded Clarion National Bank fifteen years ago.

Joseph's family were the first settlers in the Clarion area and had built a large farm where they bred and raised horses. As more people settled in the area, the town of Clarion was born, named for the founding family.

Joseph was third-generation and inherited his love the for the town and the people from his family. He had years of experience with major financial institutions and in his late forties opened Clarion National Bank to serve the residents locally. Over the years, the bank grew steadily to thirty-five branches and one-and-a-half billion dollars in assets. It had an excellent reputation for systems and service. It was loved by the people of

Clarion.

Matthew Oliver was eighteen years old when the bank was opened. During his college years at Drexel University, he worked in the Summer Management and Finance Co-op Programs at the bank. As a college graduate, he was hired to work in the Accounting Department. Over the following years, he was mentored by Joseph Clarion, promoted many times and finally became the Chief Financial Officer. Matthew liked his job immensely. He had learned so much from Joseph. He felt the bank was ideal for Clarion. The bank was committed to the community with service and performance and its goal was to make the customers say 'wow!'

But Matthew was not happy about the bank being sold and hoped that the stockholders would not approve the acquisition. He had been in touch this morning with the Greenly Brokerage Firm's manager for the Clarion stock to obtain more information. He was told the stockholders must be notified both of the potential sale and of their responsibility to vote 'yes' or 'no' for the process. He requested a complete listing of all stockholders and the value of their holdings. He knew that Joseph held twenty-five percent of the bank stock and he held five percent himself. That left twenty-one percent needed to stop the sale.

With the Clarion Bank stockholders' tasks

finished for now, Matthew got back to his daily routine. About a half-hour later, Sam appeared at Matthew's office door. "Hi, Matt. "I need about twenty minutes of your time. Are you available?"

Matthew said, "Sure, come on in."

"I need to talk with you about some technical aspects of the acquisition," Sam said.

As they spoke, it was obvious that both felt very strongly against the pending sale. Sam told Matthew about the recent meetings to stop the sale and asked him to be part of the newly developed steering committee. Matthew also said he thought Adrianne Paul would be an invaluable addition to the group.

"Adrianne Paul? She works for First City, right? Are you sure she's a good choice for our group?"

"I'm positive," Matthew said.

CHAPTER NINE

Adrianne agreed to become involved. She would be on the Steering Committee to stop the upcoming merger. Although she worked for the acquiring bank, Adrianne was strongly opposed to the sale.

Eight years ago, Adrianne at age thirty came to Clarion from New York City to work for First City Bank. She was tired of living in the big city and wanted to live in a smaller community. She applied for the Operations Manager job, was interviewed, and hired. Over the years, she worked hard, became invaluable and was now Executive Vice President of the bank.

Adrianne's start in life was not easy or planned. Adrianne was lucky to be adopted at birth; she never knew her real parents. Adrianne's mother died during childbirth, and she had no idea who her real father was. She had wonderful adoptive parents who loved her dearly. She was not told of her adoption until she was eighteen years old.

Her parents were financially well off and loved living in New York City. Her father had his own small company which was quite successful. The company management felt morally responsible to treat their employees well and fairly. The company was respected and generally well-known for all their good business practices.

Adrianne's adoptive parents along with loving her, raised and guided her well. She graduated from college at the top of her class. Her future path became working for financial institutions. Her choices were brokerage or banking. She chose banking, starting a job right after her college graduation as a Management Trainee.

Then, having tired of the fast-working pace of New York City, she moved to Clarion. It took her several months to settle in. She loved her new job and community. She had started a new life!

As part of her job, she attended monthly Chamber of Commerce meetings. At these get-togethers, business leaders congregated with each other. She was pleasantly surprised at one of these occasions to meet Maurice Paul, who worked for a New York brokerage firm that had recently opened an office in Clarion. Adrianne and Maurice were immediately attracted to each other. After a year of getting to know each other, Maurice proposed. They married six months later. Now happily married, her life was wonderful! Adding sex and true love to her life was very appealing.

She was now pleased to be working with the Clarion residents and banking personnel who were committed to maintaining the independence of the Clarion National Bank. Bring this on! Her dedication to the fair treatment of employees and customers was inbred in her character and was extremely important to her.

CHAPTER TEN

And so, it began—the plan to stop the acquisition of Clarion National Bank by First City Bank. Tom felt the thoughtful selection of the seven-person steering committee was going to be a key factor in their success. Each had integrity, a strong sense of purpose and good business ethics. They were a cross-section of perspectives, with employees from the two banks as well as members of the Clarion community.

The committee members all strongly agreed that this acquisition was a major mistake, especially since it would leave at least sixty people without work.

With a locally owned and operated community bank, the focus is on the financial needs of the families and businesses in the area. Employees often reside in the communities they serve. By contrast, a large commercial bank accepts deposits from the public and gives loans for profit. Their customer base can be any place in the world. Customer service is usually based on account size and is much better for large dollar accounts. Many of the world's largest banks have not learned their lessons; they are only too glad to accept dirty money to make more fees. These crimes are only possible when bad actors in the financial system look the other way and put profits ahead of following the law.

The seven-person committee to stop the sale met at the Clarion Union Hall three days following the sale announcement. They gathered in the main meeting room with Matthew Oliver starting the meeting talking about the responsibility of Clarion Bank to its stockholders in the sale.

"All stockholders must be notified about the possible sale of their company and the voting date required for them to approve or disprove the transaction," he explained. "Today, the Greenly Brokerage Firm delivered to me a complete listing of stockholders who own seventy-six thousand shares. The bottom line is, we need a 'no' vote for at least fifty-one percent of these shares."

The group nodded as they followed along with Matthew's explanation. "The economics of the situation are that there are two sides to this story. The senior management of the bank who voted to sell the bank and who are heavily invested in its stock are one side, and the Clarion people who want to maintain the operation as-is are the other side. This will be a real battle. We must have no less than thirty-nine thousand shares of stock voted 'no' to stop the sale. Off the top of my head, I know that nineteen thousand shares are owned by Joseph Clarion and myself. That means we need a minimum of twenty-thousand more."

After Matthew finished his presentation, the group held a discussion during which they decided that a special committee would be needed of at least twenty-three people to whip-this-vote. Art, Carolyn and Sam Van Arsdale would be in charge. They were all aware of how critical this endeavor was and eagerly agreed to start immediately. They left the room to begin planning in another area.

The four persons remaining in the group discussed a strategy of meetings, including with the Clarion Newspaper Editor and the Senior Officer for Legal Investigation at First City Bank, and also getting a lawyer onboard.

It was decided that Tom Ryan would meet with the Editor of the Clarion Newspaper to discuss a series of articles regarding the planned acquisition of Clarion National Bank by First City Bank. Tom believed a commitment would be made by the newspaper to provide information to their readers so that they could assist in stopping the sale.

Tom also suggested a person, Shawn Reagan, to take on the private investigation of the senior management of First City Bank. He explained that Shawn had a similar experience when his former employer, Corbet Container Corporation, was sold. Shawn was also the President of the Union, whose building they were now using to organize the stop the sale work. Adrianne and Andrew agreed to meet with Shawn as soon as he was available.

CHAPTER ELEVEN

Shawn Reagan and his beautiful wife, Marissa, along with their two children, Ava and Harper, spent the weekend camping in the spectacular Grand Canyon of Pennsylvania. Shawn loved the wondrous display and peace of nature, especially with his family. His personal character and individual constitution were kept whole by natural affection, life or reality as distinguished from that which is artificial.

The family was getting ready to leave when Shawn received a call from Tom Ryan. Tom was like a second father to Shawn. Shawn's first job was at Corbet Container Corporation and when he became a union steward, he met Tom. They went through many futile attempts together trying to save the company and became lifelong friends.

"What can I do for you?" Shawn asked. Tom briefly explained about the committee meeting and asked if Shawn was willing to head the senior management investigation. Shawn agreed and they set up a meeting for the following afternoon.

At three o'clock the next day, Adrianne walked into the Union Hall meeting room where Tom was having coffee.

"Good afternoon, Adrianne. Have a seat and join me? We can chat over some hot coffee and get better acquainted."

"Hello, Tom. Sure, I would like to talk with you." She poured herself a cup of coffee and sat across from Tom. "I guess you are wondering why I am here since I work for the acquiring bank First City. I love my job as executive vice president, but I also see that as the bank grows, it becomes more like a big city corporate entity, the opposite of Clarion Bank. Before I moved here, I worked for a large New York City bank. I know exactly what they are like. I will not support that type of establishment or contribute to making Clarion Bank part of one."

"That's what I wanted to hear," Tom said. "We are on the same side, we will work well together. Tell me, how do you like our town and the people here?"

"I love both, so different from where I lived in New York City. For some reason, I crave this type of environment."

"Do you have family in New York?"

"Yes, my parents live there. I have no siblings.

I see my parents about once a month. How about you? Is your family all here?"

"My wife died two years ago," he said. His expression clouded over. "I still miss her. We were married for a long time but never had any children."

"Oh, Tom, I am so sorry." He nodded his appreciation for her kindness. And it was clear to Adrianne from his expression that she could move on to the point of their meeting. "Before anyone else comes for the meeting," she said, "can we talk about my operations director, Andrew Morgan? He is such a wonderful person, so intelligent and charismatic, also excellent at his job and a longtime resident of Clarion. He is against this merger and will do whatever it takes to stop it."

Adrianne and Tom conferred quietly, and a few minutes later, Andrew walked into the room followed by Shawn Reagan. Tom greeted them both as well as introducing Shawn to the others.

"Now that we are all acquainted," said Shawn, "shall we begin? It is my understanding you want me to do some investigating."

"We think there is some illegal banking going on at First City," Andrew replied. "We see signs of money laundering and biased poor lending practices. We have no real proof, just suspicion. There are fines and prison penalties for this type of banking, as well as the ruination of a bank's reputation and customer appeal."

Adrianne added, "Shawn since you are not a banker, I want to fill you in on the history and explanation of money laundering that may help you in your investigation." She took a breath and began her explanation. This was information that Adrianne knew very well. "First, attempts to hide some illegal sources of money through complex transfers and transactions or through legal business deposits or purchasing investments allows this money to be cleared of its illegal origins. This is more common in large banks. Trillions of dollars worldwide are laundered each year, which creates a substantial impact on national economies.

"Second, a little bit of light humor. The term money laundering originates from the infamous gangster Al Capone's practice of using a bank account for the laundromat he owned to deposit huge sums of dirty, or illegal, money."

The group snickered a little at that bit of historical information. "Who knew it was literally money being washed?" Tom asked, grinning. "Thanks for the humor."

Adrianne smiled, pleased that they were understanding her approach. "Third, risky loan management is a definite major risk to any bank. A good way to lose money from defaulted loans."

Andrew spoke up next. "Shawn," he said, "I

will give you the names of possible suspects at First City for criminal activity, including our president. The president's work history as being president of an investment firm before he came here could be important. Also, they attend a committee regularly for worldwide banking. Can you find out the name of this group?"

"I understand yours and the community's problem here," said Shawn. "I will do my best to uncover any of these situations. This information is a certain deterrent to the acquisition of Clarion Bank. Thanks for sharing it with me. I will be in touch with you regularly until we are finished."

CHAPTER TWELVE

While driving to meet Adrianne the next day, Tom reflected on all that had happened in the ten days following the acquisition announcement.

He thought there had been a good show of community support. The Clarion Newspaper was extremely active in promoting the no-sale theme for Clarion Bank. Arnold, the Editor, was a Pulitzer Prize winner and his editorials, along with the supporting articles from his reporters, had been sensational to say the least. The newspaper was known for its support of the community, and the press coverage had people thinking and talking a great deal about the pending acquisition.

The Clarion National Bank Stockholders Communication Committee, led by the Van Arsdale family and twenty additional volunteers, had begun contacting the bank stockholders about the potential acquisition, explaining why their 'no' vote was so important. With the voting deadline only six weeks away, the committee was pleased with their progress so far.

Tom's last challenge was finding a lawyer to assist the community volunteers with their no-sale initiative efforts. He was meeting Adrianne for lunch to discuss that and also the status of Shawn Reagan's investigation.

He especially liked Adrianne and she seemed to think a lot like him too.

The manager at Brickside Restaurant greeted him as he walked in.

"Hi, Tom. How are you today?"

"I'm fine, thanks. I would like a table for two, please."

Soon after, Adrianne arrived at the restaurant.

"This is a nice treat, Tom. Lunch out is always good." Adrianne sat down at the table and ordered from the menu. "Now that we're settled in, what should we talk about first?"

"Let's talk about an attorney," Tom answered.

"Well, both banks have legal departments. Maybe we can use one of their attorneys?"

"No, I don't think that is wise because a lot of information we're dealing with is confidential," Tom said, adding, "I have someone in mind to use as an attorney. His name is Rustin Hugill. Rustin and his family are long-time residents of our community. He put himself through college and law school, and now has his own practice in

Clarion. He is a family law attorney, and his clients are the same individuals and families that are served by Clarion Bank. Family law is a legal practice area that focuses on issues involving family relationships. Rustin's clients love him. He is intelligent, knows the law well and is easy to be with. He also loves the outdoors, especially riding his motorcycles. I think you should meet him."

"I think so too. Will you arrange a meeting?"

Tom nodded that he would. "Now as far as the Reagan investigation status. Shawn has teamed up with his brother Corey, who is the Senior Vice President of Lending at First City Bank. They have a plan in place and have begun to research out-of-order transactions in the bank operations."

"Good news! It looks like we have all our bases covered. You do nice work, Tom."

"Thanks, Adrianne. We work well together. I feel like I almost know what you are going to say before you say it."

Two weeks later, Tom picked up Adrianne at her work. He had made an appointment for a consultation with Attorney Rustin Hugill. They entered the office just in time for the meeting. Tom introduced Adrianne to Rustin, they made a good connection as they addressed each other, and it seemed that they would have an effective relationship. Tom and Adrianne spent more than an hour talking about the proposed acquisition of

Clarion Bank by First City Bank and all the reasons and people who were opposed to the sale.

"I have known about the bank sale from the proposed beginning through the newspaper and word of mouth. The stockholder vote for the sale will be handled by the Greenly Brokerage Firm and the legal departments of both banks. The outcome of the sale will become official at the Clarion stockholders meeting happening in almost a month," Rustin said. "The other issue involving potential criminal activity is a different story. I strongly believe that the Chairman of the First City Bank Board, Bruce Burt, should be advised of this and for your protection, keep me in the loop. The investigation must be over before the stockholder meeting."

Tom and Adrianne agreed.

CHAPTER THIRTEEN

The Reagan brothers, Shawn and Corey, both with driven personalities, were persistent and deep thinkers, high performers and anxious to get the bank investigation job done. Corey, the oldest of the two brothers, had worked for First City Bank for over fifteen years, starting in the Lending Department and was now a Senior Vice President of that area. He was not in favor of the acquisition nor the current president. He had seen some strange lending practices done by the current president. What was needed was proof something illegal was done.

Corey was also a big history buff in his spare time and was writing a book about the Second World War.

Shawn Reagan had already talked with members of the steering committee overseeing the effort to stop the sale and had agreed to an investigation of some of the senior management of First City Bank suspected of criminal banking activity. Shawn had enlisted his brother, Corey, to be his partner in this process. The two men met and planned how they would handle this project. Gathering the pertinent information was the first step. They agreed Corey would work on lending and Shawn, with a couple of volunteers, would focus on money laundering. They would have to work fast. There were just three weeks to finish before the stockholders meeting.

Adrianne was working in her office, and because of the attorney's suggestion, she made an appointment to meet with Chairman Bruce Burt to discuss possible questionable and, maybe, criminal activity at First City. She was anticipating Bruce when he came to her office, walked in and greeted her pleasantly.

"Please sit down, make yourself comfortable," said Adrianne. "It is nice to see you. How are you?"

"I am just fine. Thank you. How is my favorite person and how can I help you?" Bruce Burt said. Adrianne was comforted by his kind tone of voice.

"What I am about to share with you is strictly confidential," she said. "You probably know that I am not in favor of the acquisition of Clarion National Bank, and I have been involved with a committee working to stop the sale. As part of the process, I have come across some potentially criminal information regarding two sections of our own bank. An attorney has also been consulted and it was his advice that I speak with you about it. A private investigation is being held concerning this, known only by a few people. If proof is found, it could be very damaging to our bank."

"I am shocked," Bruce stated. "I need to know more."

Adrianne shared with him all that she knew. "This has come to the surface with the objections of most of the Clarion community to the sale of their bank. I will give you daily updates until this is all over."

Bruce was visibly upset as he left her office soon after their discussion. All this turmoil was also too much for Adrianne to stand. It was time for her to go home and call it a day.

Almost a week later, Tom called Adrianne at work and told her Shawn and Corey Reagan wanted to share some of their activity and potential results with them.

"Since it's critical that the information remain confidential, they suggested going to Shawn's home and to bring our attorney," Tom said. "Can I pick you up at your home at seven?"

"Sure," Adrianne said, "I am available."

All three were later welcomed by Shawn into his home and directed to his home office where Corey was waiting. Corey waited for them to sit, and then began the briefing.

"We have uncovered pertinent information to discuss with you," Corey said. "First, the president and one executive manager at First City Bank belong to an organization that meets monthly called Worldwide Financial. We are in the process of investigating this group to determine what they are all about. Second, I have some proof about irresponsible lending with controversial clients and shortfalls in compliance procedures. Now, I'll turn the briefing over to Shawn for the third finding."

Shawn told them he had been in touch with the Clarion Police Chief Ken Van Kleef. "I learned that several SARs, an acronym for 'Suspicious Activity Reports,' have been turned over to the chief of police by some professionals. SAR reports alert law enforcement to suspicious transactions with possible links to money laundering. This is being investigated. All this information leads to fraud and criminality and is quite frightening for this small community. If the press gets ahold of this, it will be a nightmare and the stock for First City Bank will plunge. So, we have called you here to determine how you want to handle what we have found."

The attorney, Rustin Hugill, spoke first. "This is a dangerous situation. Not only are we talking about real criminals who, if convicted could face jail time, also the bank could be ruined if this situation played out and the press got involved. My question is: would the police accept the fact that it could all be cleaned up and the people fired? It will take a lot of work to do that and total secrecy. Is this an option?"

Tom agreed with the attorney's idea. He replied, "I think that is an excellent way to go. What does everyone else think?"

"Let's give this twenty-four hours to decide and Shawn, in the meantime, can you talk to the police chief to get his input on this?" asked Adrianne. "Can we then reconvene here again tomorrow at seven o'clock?"

Everyone agreed.

CHAPTER FOURTEEN

The next night, all five attendees of the meeting were back at Shawn Reagan's home finishing their discussion regarding possible criminal activity at First City Bank. After discussion with Police Chief Van Kleef, everyone agreed to attempt a cleanup and to keep it as simple and quiet as possible. The group decided that Shawn and Corey Reagan with the help of Chief Van Kleef should tackle this project. They were now under a time constraint of several weeks.

After this meeting, Shawn invited his guests to come to the living area and have a drink. As they were relaxing a bit, Shawn's wife and two children came in to say hello. Shawn's daughter Ava particularly liked Adrianne, she thought she was so pretty. Ava saw the beautiful locket necklace Adrianne was wearing. Ava told her that her mother had given her a locket like hers with a picture of her mother in it so she would never forget her. Ava told Adrianne that her necklace was so beautiful. "Does it have a picture in it like mine?" she asked. Adrianne was so pleased with Ava's attention.

"I'm glad you like my necklace," Adrianne said, "and yes, it has a picture of my real mother inside, and the locket is engraved on the back. I am afraid I do not know what it means. You see, my real mother died when I was born."

"I am so sorry. Can I see her picture?"

"Of course, you can."

Adrianne took off her necklace to show Ava the picture.

"She is so pretty just like you," Ava whispered.

Tom asked to see the necklace. "Oh, my god," he said, "I know this woman. I bought her this necklace."

Shawn realized that something significant was happening and nodded to his wife Marissa to take the children out of the room. Tears came to Tom's eyes.

"Your mother was Amanda Brown?" Tom asked, incredulous. When Adrianne nodded, Tom said, "I can tell you what the engraving on the back AILYT is."

"How can you know this? What does it mean?"

"It means, 'Amanda, I love you, Tom'," Tom said, and then he became visibly emotional about seeing the necklace. He excused himself from the group and walked back to the dining room. He sat down on a chair and began to cry. Shawn followed him.

"Tom, please tell me what this is all about?" Shawn asked.

Tom answered, "Adrianne's mother lived in Clarion years ago. I was so in love with her. In our twenties, we became engaged to marry, she was the love of my life. She did not like living in a small town like Clarion, she tried to convince me to move to New York City. I thought our love was so strong that she would change her mind. That did not happen. She left me a 'Dear John' letter and moved away. I tried for years after the letter to find her, to no avail. Now, after all these years, her daughter is here wearing the necklace I gave to her mother and Amanda died giving birth to her. It is almost too much to bear," Tom said.

Tom paused and looked intently at Shawn. "Was Amanda pregnant when she left here? Could Adrianne be my daughter?" Tom whispered.

Shawn agreed that this was a unique situation and wanted to help. "You need to get a hold of yourself to deal with it," he said. "Can I go and get Adrianne so the two of you can talk?"

"A good plan," Tom replied. "I will be ready."

A short time later, Adrianne came to speak with Tom. She began by telling him how badly she felt to bring him such sorrow.

"I had absolutely no idea of your involvement with my mother," she said. "I did not know my real mother and knew nothing about her life. She died when I was born. My adoptive parents did not tell me I was adopted until I was eighteen. They did know my mother's name and they gave me this necklace with her picture in it at that time."

"Your mother was a wonderful person," Tom said. "We had a great love between us in our twenties and were engaged to marry. I can tell you more details later. For now, please tell me your birth date and do you have a birth certificate?"

Adrianne said her birthday was February 9. "I was born in 1963 in New York City."

"Adrianne, your mother left here in August of 1962. According to what you have told me, she was pregnant when she left Clarion. I am just overwhelmed by all of this. Give me some time to collect myself."

More time passed in silence. Then, Tom and Adrianne decided to return to the other room. As they entered the living room area, they appeared to have somewhat returned to normal. Tom spoke up. "As you all were here during the conversation regarding Adrianne's necklace, we wanted to explain what is happening. I did buy that necklace for Adrianne's mother many years ago. We were at that time engaged to be married and were very much in love," he said.

Everyone was listening very carefully.

"When Adrianne's mother left me to go to New York City, she was almost three months pregnant according to Adrianne's birth date. We think there is a good chance we are related," Tom said.

"This has been an extremely emotional night for both of you," Rustin Hugill said. "Let me give you a break and handle the rest for you. I will order a paternity test and get the birth certificate. I think it is time to call it a night. I will be in touch with both of you tomorrow. We will soon know if you are father and daughter!"

CHAPTER FIFTEEN

Tom didn't get much sleep that night. His state of mind was characterized by emotions. Tom was absorbed with last night's conversation involving a heart locket necklace he bought and had engraved years ago for Amanda Brown. He also put a picture of her inside the locket. He deeply loved Amanda. They were engaged to marry almost forty years ago. Amanda unexpectedly left him with little notice. He was devastated and tried to find her to no avail. He never saw her again.

Given this sorry and intractable situation, it was almost unbelievable that Adrianne, the woman he was now working with to stop the bank merger, owned the necklace and was Amanda's daughter. Amanda died giving birth to her, Adrianne was then adopted. The real proof that it was the same necklace was the unusual engraving on the back of the heart locket and especially the picture of her mother inside the heart locket. "Extremely mind boggling, to say the least," Tom thought.

The tragedy of Amanda dying so young in childbirth, many years ago, left a lot of unanswered questions for Tom. "Why did Amanda leave me? Was she pregnant when she left me? Why would she not tell me she was carrying a child? Could Adrianne be my daughter?"

This event turned his world upside down and he was trying very hard to keep control of his feelings.

The next morning, he talked to Attorney Rustin Hugill who last night had promised to help with this situation. Rustin told him he had made an appointment for Adrianne and Tom to have paternity blood tests taken in a few days. He also had contacted the New York City hospital for information on getting a birth certificate. A short conversation was held on contacting Adrianne's adoptive parents. They both agreed that was Adrianne's decision.

In the meantime, Tom needed to get back to the business at hand. He was on his way to the Clarion Union Hall for a meeting with the Van Arsdale family—Art, Carolyn and Sam. It was time to determine how far along their committee was in contacting the Clarion Bank stockholders. This was an essential step in stopping the sale of Clarion National Bank.

The merger approval of both bank boards

required a stockholder approval vote to be held before the upcoming Clarion stockholders meeting. The 'no sale' campaign, an opposition to the merger approval, was being carried out by this committee as a way of informing and convincing the stockholders to vote 'no' instead of approving it.

The report from the committee was very positive about reaching its goal. The twenty-three members of the committee volunteered twelve hours per day to contact Clarion stockholders. A centralized phone center with computers had been temporarily set up for their use. People had been very responsive to their calls. Art Van Arsdale felt comfortable in saying that he was sure that all the stockholders would soon be contacted and that the vote would be 'no.' The Clarion National Bank would not be sold to merge with First City Bank.

"What wonderful news!" Tom exclaimed. "Kudos to your family and the committee for achieving the almost impossible. Thank you so much! Great job by all!"

CHAPTER SIXTEEN

Adrianne had an early morning meeting at her office with Bruce Burt, Chairman of the Board of Directors for First City Bank. Bruce knocked on her office door and wished her a good morning and told her he was glad to see her. They talked first about simple things and then got down to business.

Adrianne said the research team was working with the Police Chief Ken Van Kleef on locating money laundering accounts in the bank. "We are certain that some illegal transactions are going on and are actively seeking proof," she said. "Money laundering thrives on secrecy and banks being able to operate in the shadows without consequences. The Advisory Committee, along with the police, recently made the decision when the injustices are found the police will take over and the bank will clean up the affected accounts and fire the employees responsible. Currently, the suspected employees are the president and several executives working with him. How do you feel about this?"

Bruce said, "I am shocked there appears to be serious shortcomings in our banking system which raise grave ethical and regulatory concerns. Are you positive we can fix this and recover from it?"

Adrianne answered, "Yes, I am positive."

"Then I will do what is necessary," Bruce said.

About ten days later, the Police Chief Ken Van Kleef met with Corey and Shawn Reagan. Andrew Morgan and Attorney Rustin Hugill were also present. The criminal investigation was coming to an end. Chief Van Kleef reported that his detectives had investigated two 'suspicious activity reports' given to the police department as legal complaints. In them, there were facts about fronting money laundering at the bank. In these cases, fake business accounts were used as "fronts" to clear dirty money. One actual case cleared a million dollars in ten days.

Shawn, Corey and Andrew also had proof of fake investment money laundering and gambling. This information, along with risky lending for political purposes, was being turned over to the police. After several hours of presentations and discussion, it was determined that First City Bank was involved in money laundering and financial crime, most likely known by the Bank President.

Attorney Rustin Hugill commented that these

findings were against the law, and the fact that criminals and despots could so easily launder money was unacceptable. "What's the next step here?" he asked.

"One more thing to cover," said Corey. "The organization that the president met with regularly is called Worldwide Banking Association, a group of bankers from the U.S. and around the world. They support the acquisitions of banks, so that they become larger. Their common belief is that the larger banks are more open to financial systems that could be made to ignore certain laws and regulations and promote high-risk customers. Fits the philosophy of this president, doesn't it?"

Ken Van Kleef stated, "Yes, it does, and the next step here is to take this additional information back to my office. It will be turned over to the same detectives who worked on the legal complaints, and all will be reviewed. We will then make suggestions on how to go forward."

CHAPTER SEVENTEEN

And so, life continued in the small town of Clarion. Residents were going about their business as usual and some means of quiet had surrounded the two banks now in waiting mode.

The Clarion National Bank's stockholders meeting was a week away. A meeting of the Advisory Committee for the bank acquisition would also be held soon. The Clarion Police were completing their investigation of criminal activity at First City Bank. Adrianne and Tom had taken their paternity blood tests, and now were waiting for the results. Patience was now a virtue for all concerned.

Several days later, Ken Van Kleef, Clarion Police Chief, met with Attorney Hugill at the police station. Ken wanted to discuss the legal implications of criminal activity at First City Bank. His conversation began by discussing the proof of the money laundering and the customers involved.

The Investigation Committee had obtained the cooperation of bank employees in the Deposit area, Security Department and all the Branches, which provided documentation as to how money was laundered. Also, the names of customers involved and the fact that they were told by the First City Bank President Thomas Gentry to ignore computer warnings along with laws they knew were being broken.

"We also have proof that a local stockbroker was involved in two money laundering cases with First City Bank," the police chief said. "The broker took large amounts of cash, purchased and sold stocks and then deposited the receipts in an account at First City Bank. Another complication to this is that the broker is Adrianne's husband. He works for a Clarion branch of a large brokerage firm in New York City. Turns out, he also worked with Thomas Gentry at one time in his life."

"Before I make a recommendation to the Advisory Committee, I need to know your thoughts on all of this," Ken said to Rustin.

"We both know that money laundering is against the law. There are also mitigating factors that could reduce the seriousness of the crime. One being the difficulty in prosecution if there is not sufficient evidence. We do not know where all of the money is coming from. Is there a high level of remorse? We do know that money laundering exists, however for the good of the bank and the community I believe a warning from your police department to those involved, cleanup of the bank accounts and termination of the president is the right way to go," Attorney Hugill said.

"I agree," replied Ken. "I will advise the Advisory Committee as such. I will also keep a degree of confidentiality with the warnings. Also, Rustin, will you contact the Chairman of the Board regarding this situation?"

"Yes, I will take care of that."

Shortly after returning to his office, Attorney Hugill called Bruce Burt to share the allegations regarding the purported business practices of First City Bank. He spoke directly with him about his conversation with Police Chief Ken Van Kleef and about the conclusion of the money laundering investigation. He discussed the actions required to restore the bank to its reputation and integrity. He also shared the role Adrianne's husband played in this and asked him to tell her about her husband's actions.

Using the next hour to clear up his immediate general office business, Rustin decided he needed a change of pace to clear his mind. He left his office, went home to get his motorcycle, and took a long refreshing ride.

CHAPTER EIGHTEEN

Tom was waiting for the blood test results.

He was still emotional about the memory recall of his first love, Amanda Brown, and her death giving birth to a child so many years ago. He loved her so. They were engaged to be married. Amanda left him unexpectedly and broke his heart. He did not know she was pregnant when she left. It took him years to recover from her.

Still, he eventually fell in love again and was happily married to his now-deceased wife for many years. They did not have any children.

Then Adrianne came into his life, a banker who worked at First City Bank, she was against the Clarion merger and was on the Clarion committee to stop the sale with him. And then it happened, she wore the necklace he gave to her mother, Amanda. She was the child Amanda died giving birth to. Tom believed in his heart that Adrianne was his daughter.

Adrianne was now thirty-eight years old.

Adrianne told him she had been adopted at childbirth. She had wonderful adoptive parents who raised her and were still involved in her life. She was not told she had been adopted until she was eighteen years old. At that time, she was given her mother's necklace.

What a precious gift she is to me after all these years have passed, he thought. Although I did not know she existed for the first thirty-eight years of her life, I know now. I can love her for the rest of my life.

Toward the end of the day, a representative of the blood lab called Tom to tell him the paternity test for Adrianne was positive, his DNA and her DNA match was ninety-nine percent! Tom was Adrianne's father!

Tom had a sleepless night dwelling on the paternity test results. He got out of bed early with a new outlook on life. He had a daughter, a big change in his life. He was looking forward to establishing a relationship with her. He decided he would go to her office in the morning to see if she knew the results of the test.

Tom arrived at Adrianne's office in the late morning. Her door was closed. He was told by her secretary that she was in a meeting with the bank's Chairman of the Board. The secretary called Adrianne to tell her Tom was there and he was invited into the office. As Tom walked into the office, he was greeted by Bruce Burt. Adrianne stood by the window; she was visibly upset. Bruce explained that they were discussing the money laundering that was happening at the bank. Bruce said he was contacted by Attorney Hugill telling him the criminal investigation was over and the bank was responsible for cleaning up the money laundering.

"Adrianne's husband was involved with Thomas Gentry, our president, in promoting the laundering," Bruce said. "We believe the police are now talking to him regarding this."

Tom walked over to Adrianne and pulled her into his arms to comfort her. "I know how difficult this is, but we'll get through this together." Tom then said to Bruce, who looked shocked, "She is my daughter."

Bruce looked at them totally perplexed and thought to himself if only I had known the truth. It was then that Adrianne broke down and cried.

CHAPTER NINETEEN

The members of the stop-the-sale Steering Committee were gathering for what would likely be their last meeting. Tom Ryan and the Van Arsdale family of Art, Carolyn and Sam were already there. Still to come were Matthew Oliver, Andrew Morgan, Adrianne Paul, Shawn Reagan and Corey Reagan. Police Chief Ken Van Kleef and Attorney Rustin Hugill were also invited. Those who arrived early were engaged in light conversation while waiting for the others to come.

The last to arrive was Attorney Rustin Hugill with two bottles of champagne. He found a place at the front of the room and spoke about how pleased he was to be part of this group and to have worked together with everyone to maintain the identity and continuation of the Clarion National Bank.

"Your dedication, proficiency, multiple talents and extra efforts are responsible for the success of this committee," he said. Rustin then continued speaking, sharing the news that an unexpected, wonderful event came with this protest against the sale. He then explained the experience of Tom and Adrianne, who through an unusual and emotional situation found their new family relationship. "Let us all heartily congratulate them and drink a toast to our friends for finding each other after all these years. May I present Tom Ryan and his daughter Adrianne!"

Everyone stood up cheering, clapping and drinking champagne! When the celebrating calmed down, Tom and Adrianne enthusiastically thanked everyone for their warm wishes.

Tom then called the meeting to order. "First thing, I would like to add to Rustin's comments about our committee and to personally thank everyone for a job well done. I believe we have accomplished almost the impossible. We will know that for sure in several days when the stockholders of Clarion National Bank meet. The question is how did they vote? Will they have voted to sell the bank, or not? Matthew Oliver, can you verify for us the status of the meeting?

"Certainly," Matthew said. "The special Clarion National Bank Stockholder Meeting will be held in three days at the Clarion Hotel Conference Room at ten in the morning. All stockholders have been officially notified of the reason for the meeting, the date of the meeting and encouraged to attend. They have also received detailed instructions for voting for or against the sale of Clarion National Bank. The Greenly Brokerage Firm is responsible for accumulating and tallying the final vote. John Greenly, their brokerage firm's president, will report the results at the meeting."

Art Van Arsdale next reported on the special committee he and his family chaired to communicate with the stockholders regarding the bank sale. He said, "There were twenty-three much appreciated volunteers, twelve-hour days, and a tremendous workload. I feel this enormous effort will result in a 'no-sale' vote triumph."

Shawn Reagan then talked about the criminal investigation at First City Bank. "Again, we are talking about multiple persons involved in this major undertaking and a short period of time to bring this to fruition," he said. "The key persons other than himself were Corey Reagan, Andrew Morgan, Police Chief Ken Van Kleef with some of his officers, Attorney Rustin Hugill and bank employee volunteers. I would now like to turn this summary over to Ken Van Kleef."

"Thanks, Shawn," Ken said. "This was a very intense operation with a lot of cooperation and input from all. The outcome was a clear passage to cases of money laundering and poor lending practices in particular situations. Upon advice from the committee's legal counsel, Rustin Hugill, I can report that Andrew Morgan and the Chairman of First City Bank will clean up the money laundering account situation at the bank and the police will handle the perpetrators."

"Thank you all for your reports and your support and your dedication to our 'no-sale' campaign," Tom said. "Our committee has accomplished so much since our inception. I am so grateful. We will look forward to the results of the stockholder meeting in three days. It is now time to close this meeting."

CHAPTER TWENTY

Today was the big day, excitement was in the air. At ten this morning, the Clarion National Bank would hold its special stockholder meeting. People started arriving at the meeting site several hours early, all standing in line to check in. The verification of stockholders would take place before they can enter the large conference hall.

Tom arrived at nine with Art and Carol Van Arsdale. They were greeted by many people. Everyone was anxious to see if the bank would be saved from closing.

The meeting was called to order by James Conway, President of Clarion National Bank. He introduced Matthew Oliver, the bank's Chief Financial Officer, and Sam Van Arsdale, the Director of Operations. Next, he introduced the representatives of First City Bank, their new President Adrianne Paul, who replaced Thomas Gentry, no longer with First City Bank, Larry

White, Chief Financial Officer, and Andrew Morgan, Director of Operations.

James Conway explained that, according to the agenda, the required 'Proof of Notice of this Special Meeting' had already been given to the stockholders as well as the 'Rules of Conduct and Procedures.'

"So, now it is time for the presentation of the one agenda item: the proposal for the acquisition of Clarion National Bank by First City Bank, which has been approved by the Boards of Directors of both banks. Final approval must be given by a majority vote of Clarion National Bank stockholders," he said.

James Conway then said that some voting had already taken place electronically and some would also be done here in person if any shareholder has not voted and so desires. "Thirty minutes will be allowed for this process," he said.

Closing of the polls was formally given as the time allowed for voting expired. The anticipation of the results was very high, and there was a sense of anxiety in the room.

After the votes were tabulated, John Greenly, President of Greenly Brokerage Firm, stood at the front of the room to give the results.

"Seventy-seven percent of Clarion stock was voted 'no' for the First City Bank acquisition. Twenty-three percent of Clarion stock was voted 'yes' for the First City Bank acquisition."

He then said, with a firm voice, "The proposal is denied."

The audience stood up, cheering and clapping. Together, they seemed to be feeling the same euphoria, so happy that the impossible had happened, that goodness had prevailed!

CHAPTER TWENTY-ONE

The stockholder meeting was over, the sale of Clarion National Bank sale was voted down. Adrianne was now at home recovering from all the turmoil of the recent months. She had successfully worked to save the community bank from being ruined through a sale.

But in the process, her own anxiety had been increased as her husband, Maurice, had been investigated by the Clarion Police for money laundering between his brokerage office and First City Bank. She was shocked that he would be involved in this. The police had found him guilty and gave Maurice the choice to leave town or be charged with this criminal activity.

When she and Maurice talked about this after he had met with the police and before the stockholder meeting, Maurice told her he did not think that what he did was a crime. She answered that certainly money laundering is not legal and with all his experience he should know this.

"You took illegal cash funds, bought and sold stocks, and then transferred the funds from the sales to First City Bank deposit accounts. This action made the money legal. The amount of these transactions was close to half-a-million dollars. You were money laundering, at the bank where I am an officer! Did you think you would not be caught if your wife worked at this bank? Is that why you married me? You told me you loved me and did this behind my back, for how long has it been going on? Who were your illicit customers? What crimes did they commit?" she demanded to know.

Adrianne then went a step further and said, "Maurice, you have no choice but to leave town or possibly be incarcerated. I know you are hopeful that when you leave town, I will support you and go with you. However, there is no future for us. Please pack your things and leave."

That had happened several days ago. Maurice was gone and Adrianne was now alone.

As she now sat relaxing with a glass of wine in a lounge chair in her living area, her doorbell rang. She went to see who it was and saw her newly discovered father, Tom Ryan.

"Welcome," she said, "come in. Maurice has gone and I can use some company."

"I understand," said Tom, "do you want to talk

about it?"

"No thanks. I am all talked out on that subject."

Tom then said, "I brought some pictures of your mother that I thought you might like to see. They are in my car. Shall I get them?"

"Thank you, Tom. I would like that," she responded.

As Tom began to share his pictures, he told Adrianne about her mother, Amanda Brown, describing how he met Amanda in a local bakery where she worked part-time while attending music school during the day. She loved music and was an extraordinary pianist. Amanda lived with her grandmother in a small house outside of Clarion. Her parents were killed in an automobile accident when she was young.

"Look at these pictures. Wasn't she beautiful?" he asked. "Here is a picture of her wearing the necklace I gave her, which you now have. We were both young then, she was twenty and I was twenty-one. She was a beautiful woman with a pleasant personality. I used to go to the bakery to see her. I think I fell in love with her the first time I saw her. I started to regularly go to the bakery until I finally got up the nerve to ask her out. We became good friends and fell madly in love with each other. We started out by dating weekends and then saw each other almost every day. See how happy we were together in these photos."

Tom told Adrianne that she resembled her mother, especially her hair and her complexion. Adrianne and Tom continued to look at photos and talked about Amanda for at least an hour.

Then Adrianne said, "Tom, please tell me more about how and why she left you."

He answered, "I wish I could, but I don't know the answers to that. There was no warning, one day she left me a 'Dear John' letter and said she was going away, and I would never see her again. I was shocked and heartbroken. For a year I tried to find her to no avail. I never did see her again. It took me a long time to get over her."

"Tom, would you object if I did some investigating regarding Amanda Brown?" asked Adrianne. "After all the years that have elapsed since this happened, I don't know if I can be successful, but I would like to try,"

Tom nodded. "After all, she is your real mother, give it a shot."

CHAPTER TWENTY-TWO

Adrianne, recently named President of First City Bank, was now in an office befitting her title where she was meeting with Andrew Morgan, Rustin Hugill and Bruce Burt, Chairman of the Board, about the money laundering consequences at First City Bank.

Excessive money laundering, supported by their last president, was investigated and found to be true by the Clarion Police Department. Five million dollars had been processed through money laundering by illicit customers into First City Bank deposit accounts. "The responsibility of the bank for this crime," said Adrianne, "is to close these accounts and freeze the money for the legal process and federal regulators."

Andrew Morgan, the Operations Director, reported that the bank had been naïve about what happened. "I have done some research on money laundering and considering the dollar figure we experienced, our case is minor compared to the trillion-dollar yearly figure of the world," he said. He then went on to explain some facts about money laundering, saying "this process was done by criminals such as drug cartels, major businesses, thieves, dishonest governments, political figures and the like. Launderers followed their own rules and ignored most laws. Their motive is to legalize money and, in the process, make more."

"They are well-organized, more than we are," Andrew continued to explain. "There are bank employees who are paid well to assist them. The point I would like to make is these people are extremely dangerous to banks, especially small banks. If we do not get control of this, our bank could be ruined. I have some ideas of actions we must take. The first one is to establish a committee of key bank employees to investigate and take all actions that will be required to make our bank anti-money laundering. Training is essential for all bank employees and officers as soon as possible. These are just some of my thoughts to go forward, much more is required. I believe we are in danger here!"

Andrew stopped talking but then thought of one more thing to add. "I also want to report on the current money laundering cleanup which fell under my jurisdiction and was a major process. My people worked constantly with the police. I am happy to report we are now finished; all the specified accounts have been closed. As per our legal obligations, the money will be held and reported to the federal regulators."

Adrianne praised Andrew for a job well done. "Your intuitiveness in this situation was perfect for the situation and the bank. To start the anti-money laundering process, go forward with the committee you want to organize, and I will contact the federal regulators to provide the training," she said.

Bruce also complimented Andrew and repeated his comment for the bank to get a hold on money laundering. "This is so important that it will be discussed at the next board meeting. We will all work together on this," Bruce said.

Attorney Hugill said he was still in shock over the situation. "Not being a banker, it is alarming to me that something like this could happen, and the world totals of money laundering are shocking and frightening. Whatever I can do to help here, I will gladly do."

The meeting then ended with all the attendees committed to going forward.

CHAPTER TWENTY-THREE

Adrianne Paul and Rustin Hugill remained in her office following the money laundering meeting to discuss plans for filing for Adrianne's divorce. They were interrupted by her secretary when she knocked on the door to tell Adrianne that a bank employee, Mike Eagle, was waiting to see her. "Please show him in," Adrianne said.

Mike Eagle entered the office and said, "Hello Madame President, it is good to see you in this office."

"Hello, Mike, it is good to see you. How are you and your family?" Adrianne asked.

"We are all fine, thank you," Mike Eagle said.

"Please call me Adrianne, as you always do. What can I do for you?"

"I want to talk to you confidentially. I thought you were alone."

"Mike, let me introduce you to my attorney Rustin Hugill. You can talk in front of him. He will keep your confidence. Rustin, Mike has worked for our bank for a long time, he is a beloved security guard."

"Okay," Mike said. "Adrianne, I have a story to tell you. I heard through the grapevine that you recently found out that Amanda Brown was your real mother. Is this true?"

"Yes, I believe it is. My real mother died in childbirth. I was adopted at that time and did not know of it until I was eighteen years old. I never knew who my real mother and father were until just recently."

"Based on what you just said, I can tell you that I knew your mother well. We were good friends for most of our lives, until she died. We went to school together and our families were close. I was sworn to major secrecy years ago when she left town."

Adrianne was shocked by this information. "Why are you breaking your secrecy vow now?"

Mike answered, "Because I want you to know who she really was, and she would have wanted me to tell you. Do you want me to continue?"

"Yes, of course," said Adrianne.

Mike proceeded to tell what he knew about Amanda Brown. He described her as a lovely person who lost her parents to an automobile accident when she was a young girl. At that time, she went to live with her grandmother.

"They lived in a small house outside of Clarion not far from where I lived. We went to school together and graduated from high school at the same time," he said. "Amanda loved music; she was an extraordinary pianist. I learned this about her when she was still in high school. She had a music teacher who not only taught her piano but encouraged her to learn all about general music. When she graduated from high school, she applied to the Juilliard School of Music in New York City. She was devastated when she was not accepted. She then applied to a local music school, was accepted and worked part-time in a local bakery. It was there that she met Tom Ryan. They dated for a while and fell madly in love. He appreciated her music. After about a year of being together, Tom proposed to her, she was almost twenty years old. They were both very happy. She said yes, she would marry him.

"Shortly before this, she applied again to the Juilliard School in New York City for her third year of studying music. She did not expect to be accepted but Amanda was ecstatic when she received her acceptance letter. At this time in her life, she was young and immature, and she wanted to go to Juilliard to see where her special talent would take her. Her grandmother was also excited for her. The little bit of savings she had would pay her tuition. So, Amanda enrolled in Juilliard. She told me that she could not tell Tom because he would not understand.

"When she left for school, she had a letter delivered to Tom which said that she was going away and would never see him again. I thought this poor, but it was her decision. She kept in touch with me for three months after she went to school and that was the last I ever heard from her. There was never any talk of pregnancy.

"Her grandmother had a heart attack and died about six months after Amanda went to school. I thought for sure I would see her then, but she did not come home for the funeral. I knew then that something was radically wrong. I tried to call her at school and could never get in touch with her. It was not until the grandmother's attorney tried to settle her estate and the school was contacted to find out where Amanda was that he was told she had died. No reason was given except that they tried to reach her grandmother about her death but got no answer. The school accepted her body and she was buried in a New York cemetery. There was never any talk about how she died or that there was a baby," Mike said, concluding his story.

"How incredible and shocking your story is. I can't believe no one was ever told how Amanda died and there was a baby. I am so sad that she died like this," Adrianne said. "Mike, thank you so much for sharing this secret information and your relationship with my mother. Your story sheds some light about where she went when she left town. I must learn more about her life at school, what happened in her last six months of life."

Mike got up from his chair to leave and said to Adrianne, "I will leave and let you contemplate what I have told you. After some time has passed and you may have more information, we can talk again. I would like to share more of your mother's life with you. Nice to have met you Attorney Hugill."

After he left, Adrianne turned to Rustin and said, "I don't know what to say or feel."

Rustin replied, "I know it is difficult for you right now, but I have a suggestion. We will take a trip to Juilliard School. My friend from law school, Roderick Poore, is one of their attorneys. He has his office at the school. I can call him later today and explain the situation. Maybe if we are lucky there is someone there who would remember your mother. What is the year she went to school?"

Adrianne said, "She would have started August 1962 and my birth date was February 9, 1963."

Rustin said, "I have the information I need, and it is now time for me to leave. I will phone you later."

CHAPTER TWENTY-FOUR

Adrianne heard from Rustin the next day. He had contacted his friend Roderick Poore at Juilliard School in New York City and told him the whole Amanda Brown story. He was happy to report that there was a professor on staff who remembered her mother.

"Oh, how wonderful," exclaimed Adrianne. "When can we go there?"

"That is up to you, when are you available?"

"I will get back to you with a date," she said.

A week later they arrived at the Juilliard School and met Roderick Poore in his office. They were both happy to see him. Rustin and Roderick talked about their legal business and Rustin reminded him of their recent phone conversation regarding the reason they had come.

"Of course," Roderick said, "you will be meeting with John Ostertag, he is expecting you. Let me take you both to his office. John is a long-time employee of our music school and is now the

Director of Special Events."

They walked into his office and Roderick Poore introduced everyone and then excused himself to leave.

John said, "I believe you are looking for information on a student from many years ago named Amanda Brown."

"That is correct," stated Adrianne. "She was my mother."

"After talking with Roderick a few days ago, we looked for her file. We found it stored away with other important papers for 1962. I reviewed her information before you came. She and I came to Juilliard at the same time, I as a new instructor and she as a student. It is difficult to recall all, being that it was over thirty-eight years ago, but I do remember some things, some things in fact I will never forget," John said. "She and I were both young, probably in our early twenties. She was extremely talented. It is very rare to see a student with as much musical talent as she had. She was a wonderful pianist and I remember she played the piano at some of our special events when she came here and audiences raved about her performances, she had standing ovations from her audiences. I do remember I became very fond of her as a student. She did belong here. I also remember she was very happy here for her first several months and then she confided to me she was pregnant.

Well, back in those days a pregnant student was not allowed. The school management made an exception in her case due to her exceptional talent. They expected great things from her. She could stay until she had the baby and then they would make plans for her return.

"During her last few months here, she had a class in music production. She was excited about this class and started to write a song. She wrote the music and words to a song she called 'Love's Choices.' It turned out to be a beautiful piece of music. If you look here in her file, the finished product is here. I will make you a copy. The ending words of the song are: 'My choices of love are music and man; listen and I will tell you why. The love of music is the language of the spirit and opens the secrets of life bringing peace. The love of my man Tom isn't just something I feel it is something I become. Tom, I will love you forever with all that I am.' This song, 'Love's Choices,' was published with the anonymous name of Amanda Love and became a big hit years ago."

Adrianne and Rustin were speechless, and so John continued. "Amanda died shortly thereafter in childbirth. She asked me to be her emergency contact and as such the hospital called me to tell me when she died. How awful that was. I was heartbroken and devastated. Amanda had also given me her grandmother's phone number to call in case of an emergency. I did call the grandmother to tell her she passed away and I remember she became hysterical.

"When an official from the school called the grandmother later about transporting Amanda's body for a funeral, they could never reach her. We finally bought a casket for her body and had her buried in a New York City cemetery. We also felt some responsibility for the baby. We learned that the baby was healthy and being adopted by a wonderful husband and wife. It took me a long time to get over this. I never became that close to a student again," John said.

Tears were forming in his eyes. "Do you have any questions? What I told you is all I can recall."

"I have no questions, thank you so much for your time and sharing this information with us. What you have told us clears up many questions about Amanda's life, about my mother's life," Adrianne said.

Adrianne and Rustin left New York City soon after their meeting with John Ostertag and arrived home before dark. On the way home, she told Rustin how much she appreciated him for making this trip possible. They also discussed that she must share this information with Tom tomorrow. She was not sure how he would react. Rustin asked Adrianne if he could find for her a record or DVD of her mother's music.

"Rustin that would be wonderful, thank you!"

The next evening Tom came to Adrianne's home at her invitation, to talk about her mother. She reminded him of her desire to find out more about her mother after she left Tom. She told him of her first meeting with Mike Eagle who came to her office to tell her how Amanda had sworn him to secrecy about where she was going after Tom's 'Dear John' letter. She then talked about Rustin and she going to Juilliard Music School to meet with John Ostertag who remembered Amanda as his student. She shared with Tom what he talked about for over an hour recalling her time at the school. "His discussion was very poignant, going from when she arrived to ultimately her death," Adrianne told Tom.

Adrianne then gave Tom the copy of the song her mother wrote. He lost control when he read it. After some time passed, Tom recovered and he said, "It is now time to put this all behind us and move forward. The last thing we will do for your mother is to bring the casket with her remains home and be buried next to her parents and grandmother."

Adrianne and Tom agreed to get back to banking and make their banks the best in the country.

EPILOGUE

Several months passed and many changes occurred due to the failure of the Clarion National Bank acquisition.

The presidents of both banks were gone. First City Bank fired its President Thomas Gentry for criminal activity and then named Adrianne Paul the new President to replace him. James Conway, President of the Clarion National Bank, resigned along with several bank officers and board members. Joseph Clarion came out of retirement to take his place as president.

Tom Ryan was surprised and pleased to be elected as Chairman of the Clarion National Bank Board.

The new relationship of father and daughter between Tom and Adrianne was growing into one of reality. Tom was ecstatic. Adrianne and Tom were pleased to have learned about the last six months of her mother's life.

But Adrianne also became saddled with another problem. Her husband had left her to go back to his prior job in New York City. Maurice Paul was found by police to be involved with money laundering at First City Bank. His choice was basically to leave town or be prosecuted. Attorney Rustin Hugill had helped her get through this awful situation. Adrianne filed for divorce.

Art and Carolyn Van Arsdale from the Steering Committee were asked to be on the Clarion National Bank Board of Directors. Carolyn declined, but Art was pleased to accept. Sam Van Arsdale was promoted to Executive Vice President in charge of Bank Operations.

Other members of the Steering Committee also had changes in their lives. At First City Bank, Andrew Morgan became Executive Vice President in charge of Bank Operations. Corey Reagan was promoted to Executive Vice President of Lending. Shawn Reagan was asked and accepted to be a member of the Bank's Board of Directors.

Matthew Oliver was being mentored by Joseph Clarion to be considered for a future presidential position at Clarion National Bank.

It was important for Tom as new Chairman of the Clarion National Bank Board to replace the five Board of Director members who resigned. He understood and believed that the board governs while the staff manages and these are separate, yet fully aligned, functions. He wanted an effective back-to-the-basics board with the characteristics of being strategic, mission-centered, diverse, professional, collaborative and committed. Considering all this, his first choice was Michael Knight, a Divisional President for a local Hathaway Company. Next were Attorney Rustin Hugill, the attorney for the 'no-sale' Steering Committee, and Carol Baker, a health care professional, and also, Ken Van Kleef, Clarion Chief of Police, and Jeannie Moore, a major stockholder. All these persons accepted Tom's nomination to be Board Members.

All these changes created positive feelings in both banks, so positive that employees suggested to both Bank Officers that a Celebration Party was needed. Both presidents proudly agreed.

A committee of representatives from both banks was assigned the responsibility of planning the party. The Clarion Newspaper advertised the party with an open invitation for all residents.

As the party date got near, the newspaper had an article regarding the Editor in Chief, Arnold Baker, who was again nominated for a Pulitzer

Prize—this time for his articles about the proposed acquisition of the town's bank and the almost impossible fight to stop it. This recognition was another reason to celebrate.

As all the plans came into place, it was time for the party to begin. Two Clarion fire engines with sirens blaring came through the town to celebrate the occasion. The Fire Chief, Ken Andrzejewski, and his wife Chris, were some of the first townspeople to arrive at the party.

The greeters for the party were stationed at the door to the Banquet Hall of the local hotel, where they Celebration Party was being held. They were Bruce Burt, Chairman of First City Bank Board and his lovely wife, Patti. Next to her was Adrianne, President of the same bank. Then came Tom Ryan, Chairman of the Clarion National Bank Board, and father to Adrianne. On his side was Joseph Clarion, President of the same bank. These people greeted the guests. Five hundred were expected.

Among the guests were the Mayor of Clarion, Gary Amster, and his wife Nancy, along with all the Board of Directors members from both banks. Some were with their spouses, Carol with Anthony Rissi, Kay with Robert Van Zyl, and Mark McFall with his beautiful wife Cindy.

Talk was light, happy and complimentary. Most of the employees and customers of both banks were there, as were the town's residents. Everyone took the opportunity to socialize with each other and to have a good time.

After two hours of welcoming guests, the greeters were greatly surprised by the last guests to arrive: Jerry Rackoff, the U.S. Senator for their area with his assistant, Jeremy Woodside. They were pleased to be part of the celebration and also to recognize the success of everyone's efforts. At this point, the greeters entered the party with the senator in tow.

Rustin Hugill came for Adrianne with a drink for her and a present for her father, an actual recording of her mother's hit song. They then began to socialize.

At the same time, Bruce and Tom went to the stage to welcome all and say a few words.

Bruce said he was pleased to welcome everyone to the Celebration Party and then talked about the reorganization of his bank. "This all happened because indirectly you showed us what we needed to be," he said. "More customer-oriented, more accommodating and supportive. We eliminated wrongful practices. We are now a very proud and stronger financial institution. Thank you!"

Tom then said, "From my heart, I thank all of you for everything you did to keep our bank from being acquired and saving a lot of people's jobs. It was very near impossible to beat the corporate executives who stood to make a lot of money by buying our bank, but we succeeded. To put it simply, it was Greed versus Goodness! I am so proud of all of you and what was accomplished. We knew we didn't want our lives to change in that way. We will continue to live in a wonderful small town where people take care of and like each other. The goodness in all of you has prevailed! Thank you!"

THE END

ABOUT THE AUTHOR

In her debut novel, *If the Truth Be Known: Greed Versus Goodness*, Sara Singleton tells a story that blends her love of family and community with her expertise in banking gained from a nearly three-decade career. Sara was born, raised and still lives in eastern Pennsylvania.

Made in the USA
Middletown, DE
09 December 2022

17831949R00073